# THE SALON

BY Nick Bertozzi

 St. Martin's Griffin ≋ New York

www.stmartins.com
Library of Congress Cataloging-in-Publication Data Available Upon Request
ISBN-13 978-0-312-35485-5
ISBN-10: 0-312-35485-1
First Edition: April 2007
10 9 8 7 6 5 4 3 2 1

For Kim

3

4

5

12

13

14

15

17

22

23

24

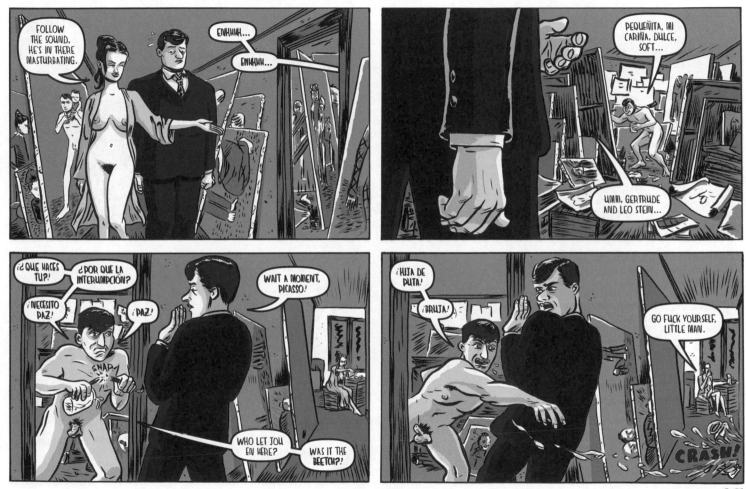

25

26

27

32

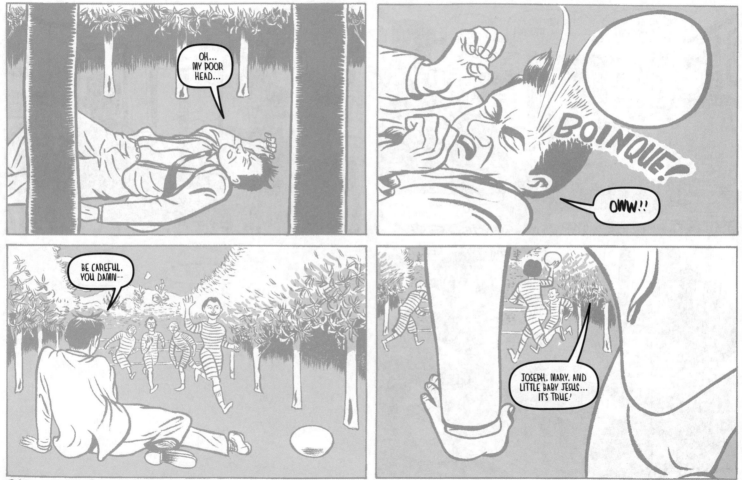

34

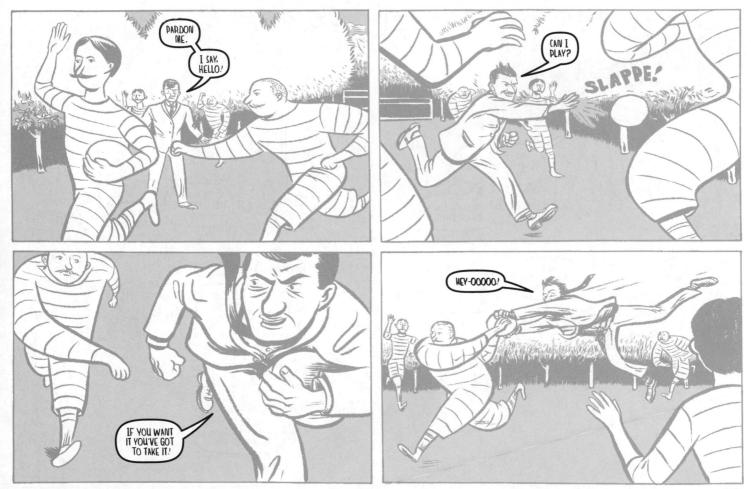

35

38

43

45

46

47

48

50

55

56

58

59

60

62

63

64

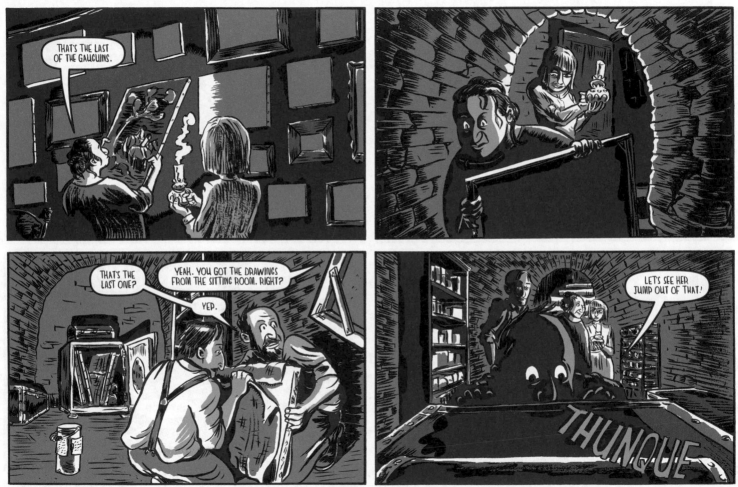

65

67

69

70

77

78

83

85

86

88

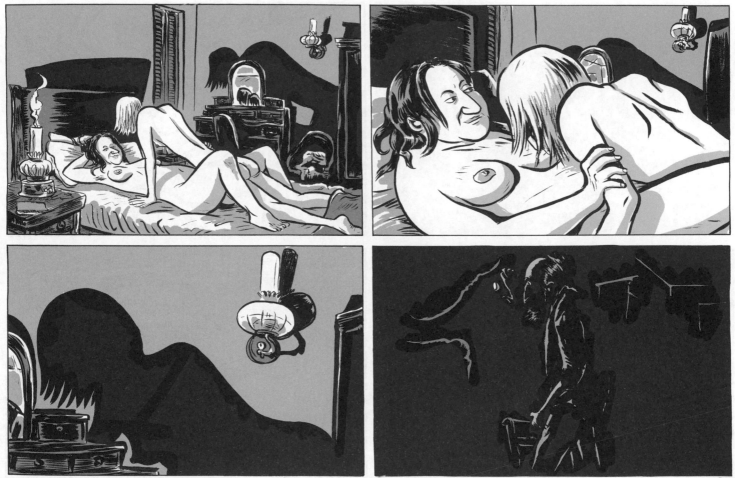

98

99

102

104

107

108

109

113

114

115

116

122

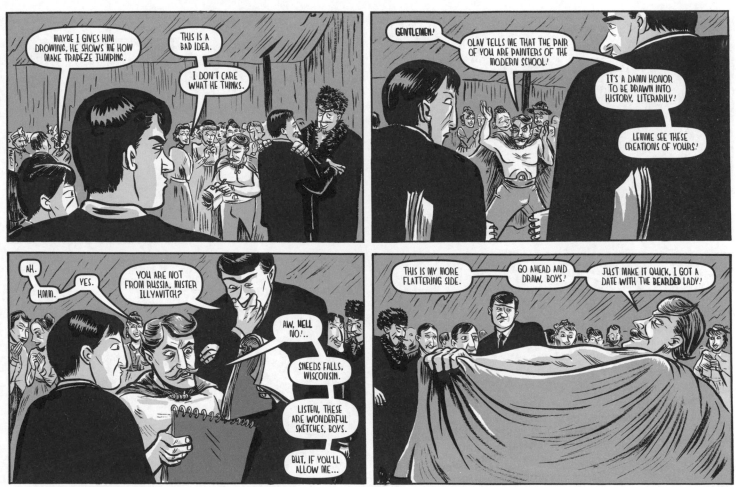

123

125

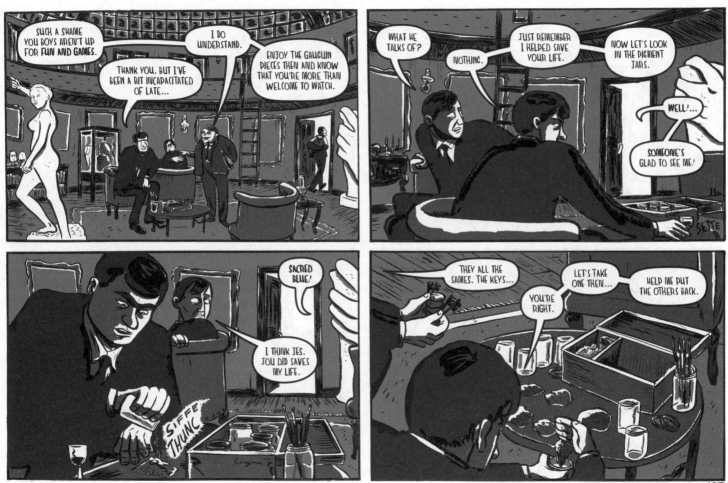

127

133

134

138

139

140

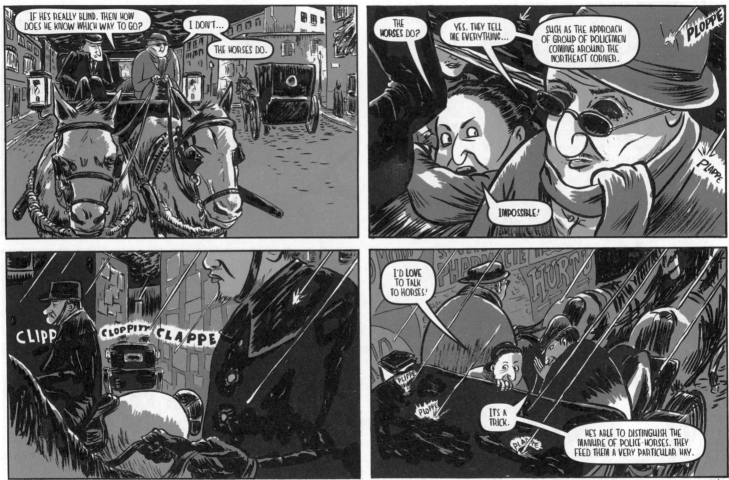

141

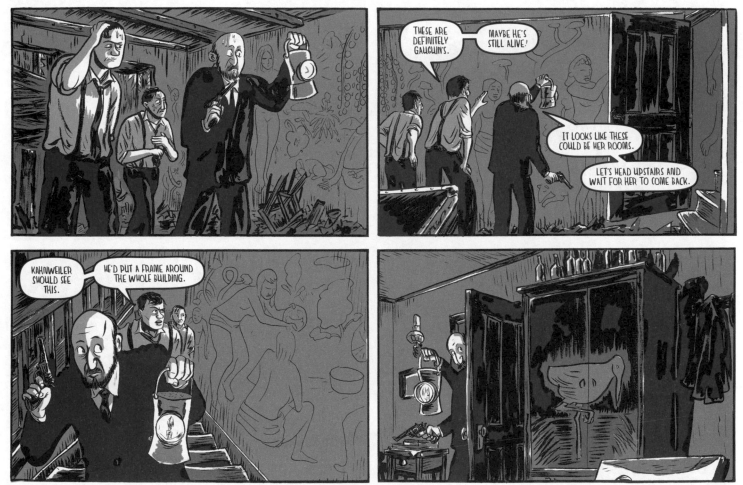

143

144

147

149

150

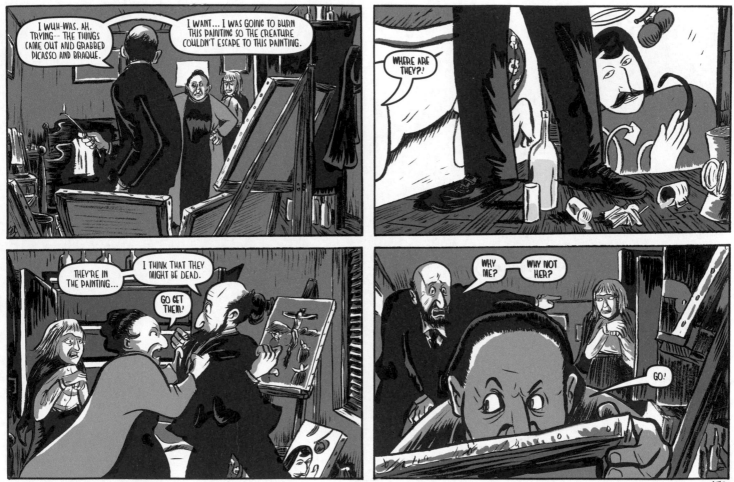

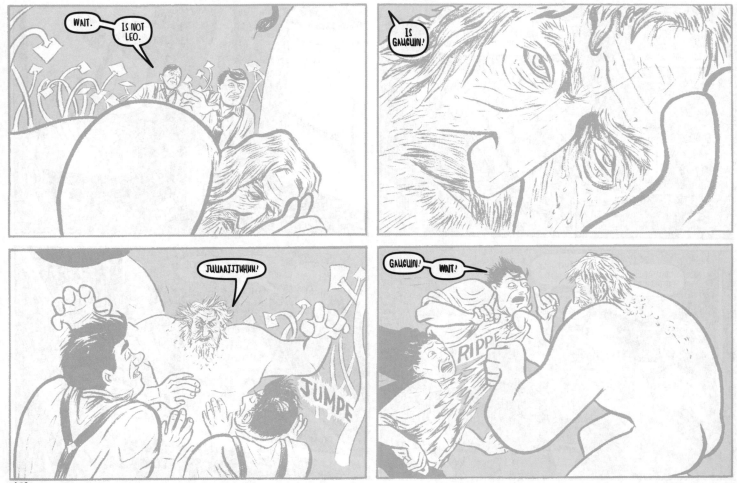

153

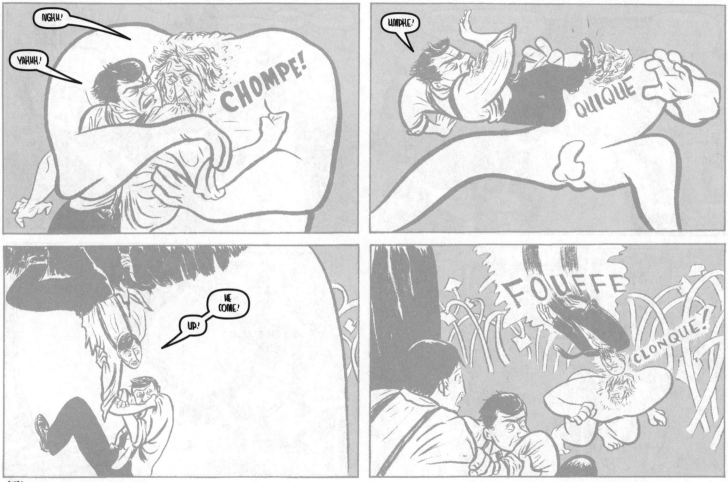

154

157

159

160

163

164

169

173

174

177

178

THE END.

THANKS TO:

Kim Chaloner, Dean Haspiel, Michael Homler, Jason Little, Jeff Mason, Tanya McKinnon,

Jessica Abel, Jonathan Ames, Darin Basile, Josh Bayer, Gabrielle Bell, Greg Bennett, Sabina, Vanessa, Lula, Julia, Edward, and Judith Bertozzi, Chester Brown, Ted Chaloner, Scott Cohn, The Comic Book Legal Defense Fund, Ryan D'Angelo, Glenn Davis, Bob Fingerman, Glen David Gold, Myla Goldberg, Tom Hart, David Heatley, Alex Holden, Dan Holloway, Susan Krausz, Gordon Lee, Andrew Lis, Matt Madden, Joey Manley, Josh Neufeld, Christine Norrie, Charlie Orr, Dennis Pacheco, Gary Panter, Paul Pope, Bill Rees, Gabe Soria, Michael Storrings, James Sturm, Dave Wallin, Lydia Walshin, and Mary-Lou Watson.